Little Ant
and the Spider

S.M.R. Saia

Illustrations by Tina Perko

Little Ant had two best friends. Buddy Ant and Tiny Ant were not the most popular ants in the anthill, but like Little Ant, they were strong and smart and quick. They worked hard, and there was no one with whom Little Ant would rather hoist a crumb.

One day, Little Ant and his friends were playing kick the crumb after a hard day's work, when another group of ants approached them. Little Ant greatly admired these three ants. They were big, and they were popular. When they stopped for a moment to watch the game, Little Ant said, "Do you want to play with us?"

Bully Ant, who was the biggest of them, laughed. "We are too big to play kick the crumb," he said.

"We are going on an adventure," the second ant said.

"We are going to the far end of the field," the third ant explained, "to look at the spider."

Little Ant's eyes grew wide. "No ant is allowed to go near the spider's web," Little Ant said.

Bully Ant laughed. "The web isn't really sticky," he said. "That's just a story that the grown-up ants tell to keep us away."

"Why would the grown-up ants want to keep us from the spider web if it isn't dangerous?" Little Ant asked.

"The spider is wise," Bully Ant answered. "If we go talk to the spider, then we will learn things, and we won't need the bigger ants anymore."

"Well, we are not allowed to go," Little Ant said.

"You're just scared," Bully Ant taunted. "They are going to call you Little Ant for the rest of your life, because you will never have courage, and you will never be wise."

"Don't pay attention to them," Buddy Ant said when the bigger ants were gone.

"They will only get you into trouble," Tiny Ant agreed.

Little Ant thought about this. He did not like being little. He did not like being told what to do and what not to do. What if what Bully Ant had said was true, and the spider was wise? What if every ant did have to confront his fear of the spider in order to grow up?

It bothered him so much that he asked Uncle Ant about it. "The spider is very dangerous," Uncle Ant told him. "She sets a trap for unsuspecting insects. The spider would love to have a Little Ant for breakfast, I am sure."

"Some of the other ants say the spider is wise," Little Ant said.

"Maybe she is, and maybe she is not," Uncle Ant replied. "But no ant with any sense is going to get close enough to find out."

The next time Little Ant saw Bully Ant and his friends, he told them what Uncle Ant had said, but they were not convinced. "We went to the spider's web yesterday, and nothing bad happened to us," Bully Ant said.

"We are tired of the grown-up ants telling us what we can and can't do," the second ant said.

"We are going to keep going back until we get to talk to the spider," the third ant said. "You should come too, Little Ant."

Little Ant thought and thought and thought. He did not want to disobey Uncle Ant. But he wanted to find out the truth for himself.

"Okay," Little Ant said, with a tremor in his voice. "I will go with you."

It was a long walk to the spider's web, long enough for Little Ant to second-guess himself. But he was a little excited, too. He wondered what wise thing the spider might tell him. He wondered how the bigger ants would treat him, once they heard that he, Little Ant, had gone to see the spider, and had brought some of her wisdom back with him.

"It's not far now," Bully Ant whispered.

The blades of grass seemed to get closer and closer together as they went on, and the sun slipped behind the clouds. Little Ant shivered in the shade. Soon, they stopped. The web stretched out before them, its many fine strands anchored between the stalks of two great plants.

Bully Ant nudged Little Ant's shoulder. "Go ahead, Little Ant," he said. "Go and see if the spider is at home."

Trembling with fear and excitement, Little Ant climbed up one of the stalks and carefully stepped onto a strand of the web. It quivered beneath his weight as he put another foot and then another in front of him. Each step was harder to take than the one before. By the time he had reached the center of the web, he found that he was unable to lift his feet at all.

Little Ant called down to the other ants in a panic. "Help me!" he cried. "I'm stuck!" The web moved beneath him again, and Little Ant looked back over his shoulder to see the spider's head emerge from the shadow of a leaf. "Bully Ant! Help me to get loose!"

But the three bigger ants had also seen the spider. Little Ant watched, helplessly, as they ran away, leaving him behind.

Then Little Ant heard the spider's voice. "Why are you here?" she asked. "I rarely get ants in my web."

Little Ant dug down deep and answered her with his very last bit of courage. "I wanted to talk to you. I am ready to grow up."

The spider laughed. "Getting yourself caught in a spider's web is a funny thing to do if you want to grow up," she said.

The spider raised one leg, and then another. Little Ant felt the vibrations in the strands as the spider moved closer and closer to him. He looked for the other ants, but they were nowhere to be seen. Had they gone for help? Oh, how he hoped they had gone for help!

"I heard you are wise," Little Ant said.

"I know a few things that you don't know, anyway," the spider said, moving even closer to Little Ant.

"Like what?"

"Like this," the wise spider said, and she whispered her secret into Little Ant's ear.

Then, with one quick move, she snipped first one strand, then another, until Little Ant was free. He dropped to the ground, surprised and trembling. "I have already had breakfast," the spider said, "so I'm going to let you go. But remember what I told you." Little Ant nodded. Then he turned and ran.

He had not gone far when he ran into Buddy Ant and Tiny Ant. "What are you doing here!" Little Ant cried. "The spider is close!"

"We saw Bully Ant and the others come running back to the anthill without you," Buddy Ant explained. "We thought you might need help."

"Thank you," Little Ant said. He threw his arms around his friends' shoulders and added, "The spider was wise, but she didn't tell me anything that I shouldn't have known all along."

"You were right about the spider," Little Ant told Bully Ant and the others when he got back to the anthill. They begged him to tell them what wise thing the spider had said.

"She told me that my real friends will not desert me at the first sign of trouble," Little Ant told them. Then he went to join his real friends in a game of kick the crumb, perfectly content, for the time being, to remain one of the little ants.

Free activities for the Little Ant books are available at
http://littleantbooks.com.

Follow Little Ant on Facebook and Instagram at @littleantnews. Learn more
about Little Ant's life; be the first to know when there are new Little Ant activities
available for free download, and get cool news about insects you can share
with your kids!

Published by Shelf Space Books
http://shelfspacebooks.com

ISBN: 978-1-945713-26-2

Made in the USA
Middletown, DE
29 July 2019